THE BRAVE COWBOY

THE BRAVE COWBOY

Written and Illustrated by

JOAN WALSH ANGLUND

Andrews McMeel
Publishing, LLC

Kansas City • Sydney • London

For my son Todd

First published by Harcourt, Brace and Company in 1959

The Brave Cowboy copyright © 1959, 2000 by Joan Walsh Anglund.

Andrews McMeel Publishing, LLC
an Andrews McMeel Universal company
1130 Walnut Street, Kansas City, Missouri 64106

www.andrewsmcmeel.com

12 13 14 15 16 TWP 16 15 14 13 12 11 10

Library of Congress Cataloging-in-Publication Data

Anglund, Joan Walsh.
    The brave cowboy / written and illustrated by Joan Walsh Anglund.
        p. cm.
    ISBN: 978-0-7407-0649-3
    [1. Cowboys—Fiction. 2. Play—Fiction.] I. Title.
  PZ7.A586   Br2000
  [E]— dc21   00-037984

Composition by Kelly & Company, Lee's Summit, Missouri

Once there was a cowboy.

He was strong and brave.
He was not afraid of coyotes.
He was not afraid of mountain lions.
He was not afraid of ornery rustlers.

He stood tall and straight . . . and had a two-holster belt.

Each morning he would eat breakfast . . .

brush his teeth . . .

and feed the cat.

Each day he put on his hat . . .

pulled on his boots . . .

and buckled his two-holster belt.

Sometimes, he would set out to find
a camp of rustlers to round them up
and put them in jail . . .

Or, maybe he would hunt bank robbers that might
be in the territory . . .

Or, maybe he would scare a rattlesnake . . .

or capture
an angry
mountain lion . . .

or just take a ride
across the prairie.

He was always busy.
He had much to do.
He must bring in provisions . . .

rescue fair maidens
in distress . . .

warn the stagecoach that the bridge was out.

Sometimes things went well for the cowboy . . .

when he was made deputy sheriff
by the people of the town . . .

when he led the covered
wagons across the plains . . .

when he won first prize
at the rodeo.

And sometimes he had troubles . . .

when his tent collapsed while he was camping out . . .

when he ran out of food on the
trail, far away from camp . . .

when his horse went lame while he was hunting buffalo . . .

But he was never baffled . . .
he was not afraid . . .
and he never gave up.

And so, when night fell on the prairie
and the coyotes howled at the moon,
the tired cowboy . . .

took off his boots . . .

hung up his hat . . .

and unbuckled his two-holster belt.

He said his prayers . . .
climbed in his bunk . . .

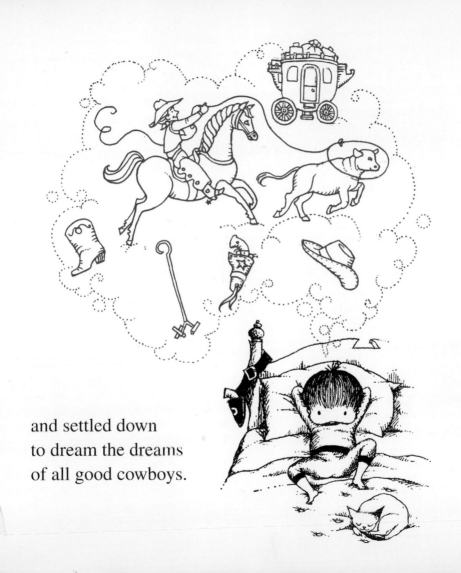

and settled down
to dream the dreams
of all good cowboys.

Good night little cowboy . . . Sweet dreams.

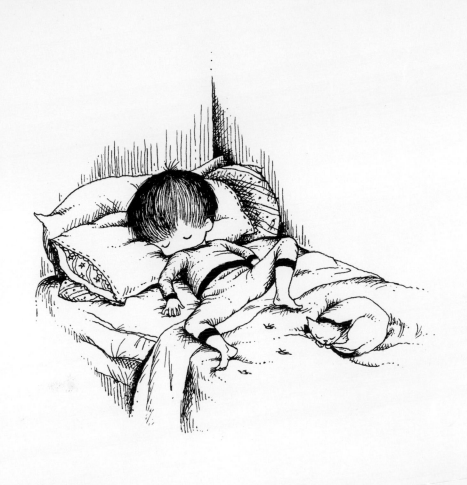